flossie

Trevor

ERIC

ernie

For Joel
(who gave me the idea)

and Hannah
(because it was her rat)

JANETTA OTTER-BARRY BOOKS

Enormouse copyright © Frances Lincoln Limited 2013
Text and illustrations copyright © Angie Morgan 2013
The right of Angie Morgan to be identified as the author
and illustrator of this work has been asserted by her
in accordance with the Copyright, Designs
and Patents Act, 1988 (United Kingdom).

First published in Great Britain in 2013 and in the USA in 2014 by
Frances Lincoln Children's Books,
4 Torriano Mews, Torriano Avenue,
London NW5 2RZ

www.franceslincoln.com
All rights reserved

A catalogue record for this book is available from the British Library.

ISBN 978-1-84780-448-8

Illustrated with watercolour, pastels and collage

Printed in China

1 3 5 7 9 8 6 4 2

ENOR M OUSE

ANGIE MORGAN

F

FRANCES LINCOLN
CHILDREN'S BOOKS

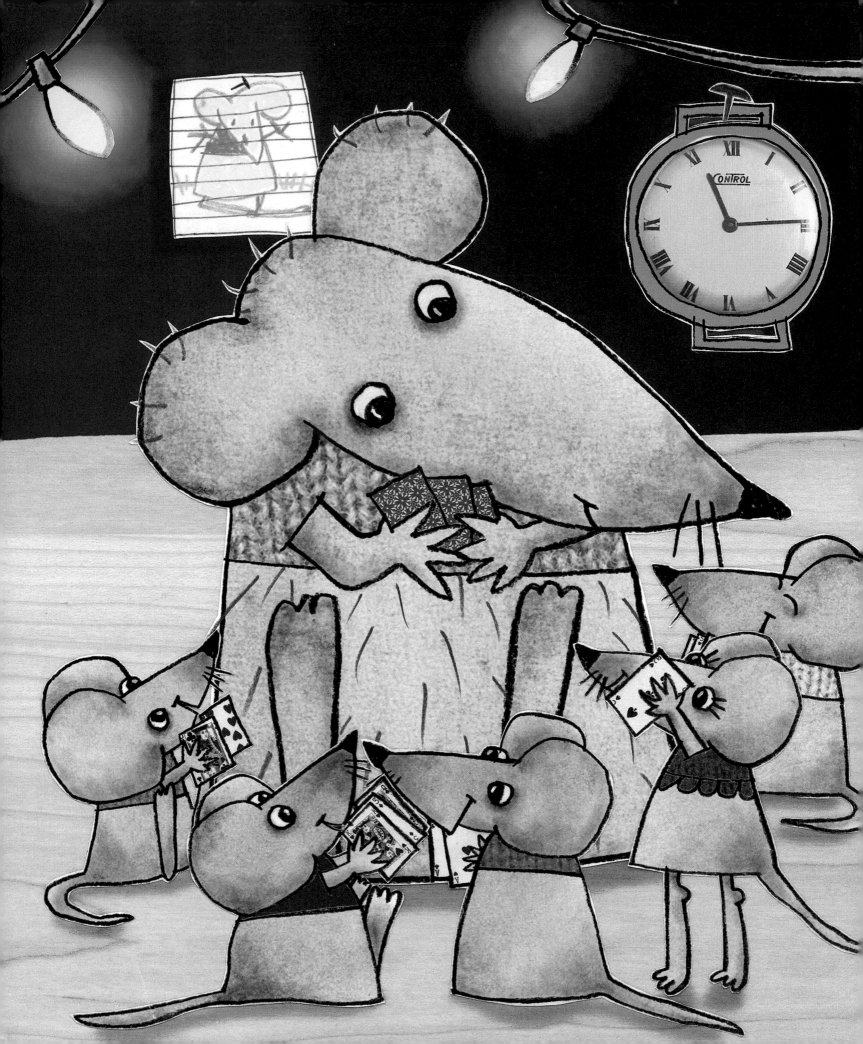

...mouse was...

BIG.

He didn't know why.
He just was...

really BIG.

His best friend Tinymouse
tried to help.

"Don't worry, Enormouse.
Being big isn't SO bad."

And it wasn't.
Being big was
really quite useful.

When he went exploring
with the other mice
he could reach things
they couldn't reach.

He could lift **REALLY** heavy cheese.

He could carry the little mice when their legs got tired.

RATS
The Common Rat
(Rattus Norvegicus)

Rats are **bigger** than
long snouts, coa
scaly tails. They like
or rubbish dump
find their foo
anything a
food that is
overed wi

One day, when Enormouse
was exploring with Tinymouse,
they came across a large book.

The two friends looked at
the pictures. They looked
at each other.

"I think I know why you're
so big, Enormouse.
You're not a mouse at all...
You're a **RAT!**"

MICE
The House Mouse
(Mus musculus)

Mice are smaller than **rats**. They have pointy snouts and shiny **black eyes** like beads. They have **large ears** and soft **fur**. They **steal** their food

from **humans** and especially like **chocolate** and **apples**. They make their **homes** under **floors** or in garden **sheds** and they keep them very **clean** and **tidy**.

...ice. They have
...e fur and
...o live near **dustbins**
... which is where they
... They will eat
... they **specially like**
...ouldy and **smelly** and
...flies.
...enerally **friendly** but have
...ners and **never** say please

Being a rat was rather a shock.

"I don't think I belong in the
Mouse House any more,"
he said to himself sadly.

"I think I should go and find
some rats to live with."

So Enormouse left the Mouse House.

At first he felt afraid and rather lonely.

But a friendly rat came by who kindly took him to the Rats' House.

When they arrived
Enormouse was horrified.
There was mess EVERYWHERE!

RATS' HOUSE

Pleez
nock

It wasn't messy like an untidy bedroom.
It was MUCH worse.
It was a MOULDY, SMELLY,
BUZZING with FLIES sort of mess.

The smell was so bad it made
Enormouse's eyes water.

He thought he ought to ask
if they would like him to
do a spot of cleaning.
But the rats only laughed.

Poor Enormouse. He just wasn't
like the other rats. His heart ached
for Tinymouse, his other mouse
friends and his cosy home.

He began to think he had been a bit hasty.

Back at the Mouse House the mice were all VERY sorry that they had laughed at Enormouse.

So they all
set off bravely.

None of them had the
faintest idea where
they were going...

...and soon they were all
very, very lost.

In the Rats' House, Enormouse finally knew what he had to do.

He said goodbye to the rats, thanked them politely for having him, and set off home.

"GOODBYE!"

Meanwhile, in the dark,
the mice were very frightened.

They began to hear strange
and scary noises all around.

An owl hooted in a tree.

"HELP!" they squeaked.
"We're all going to die!"

Suddenly they heard footsteps
approaching and a LARGE
shadow LOOMED over them.

There was much trembling
and squeaking and a small
voice said...

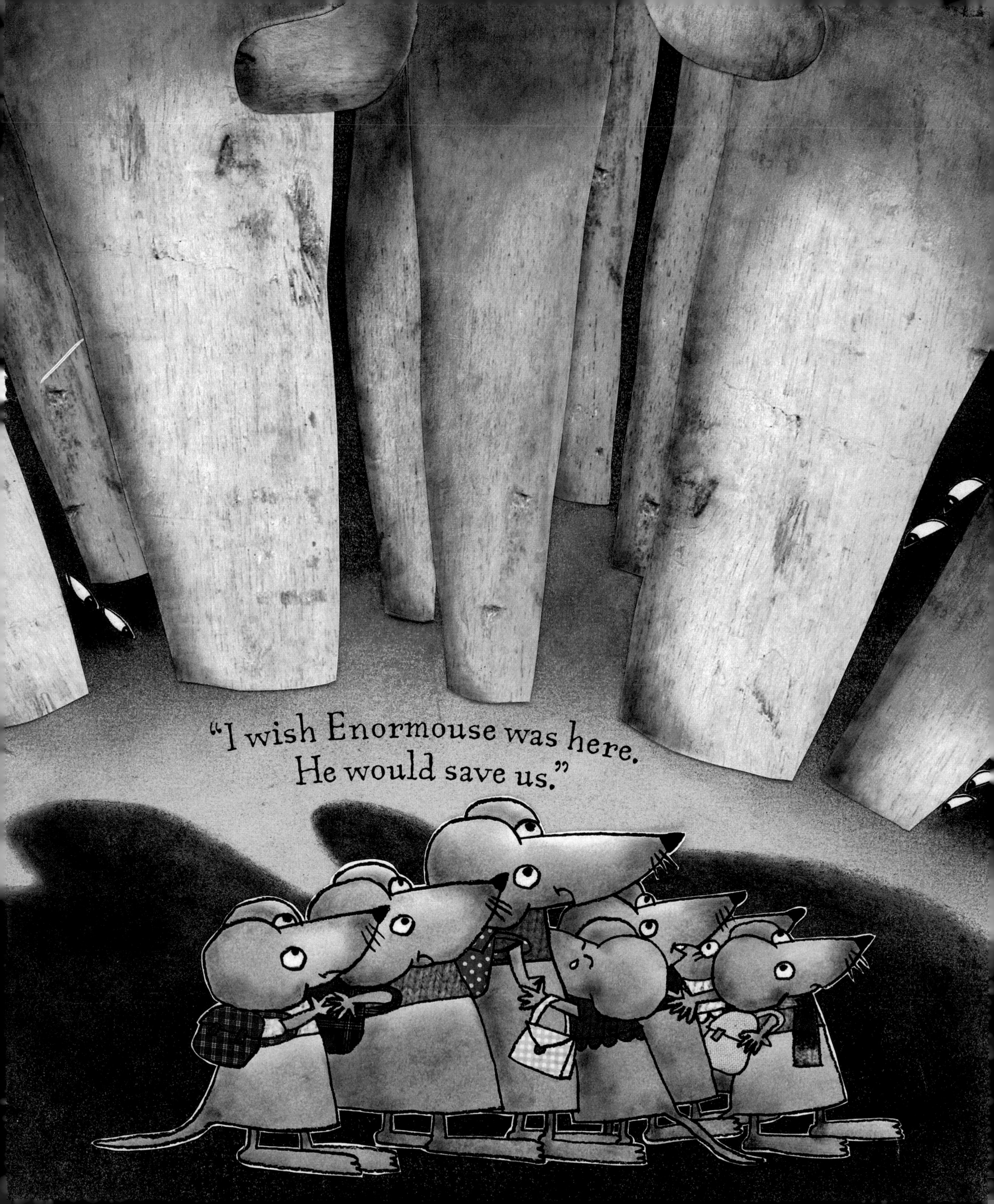

"I wish Enormouse was here.
He would save us."

And out of the darkness
a familiar voice said,

"I AM here!"

It was Enormouse!

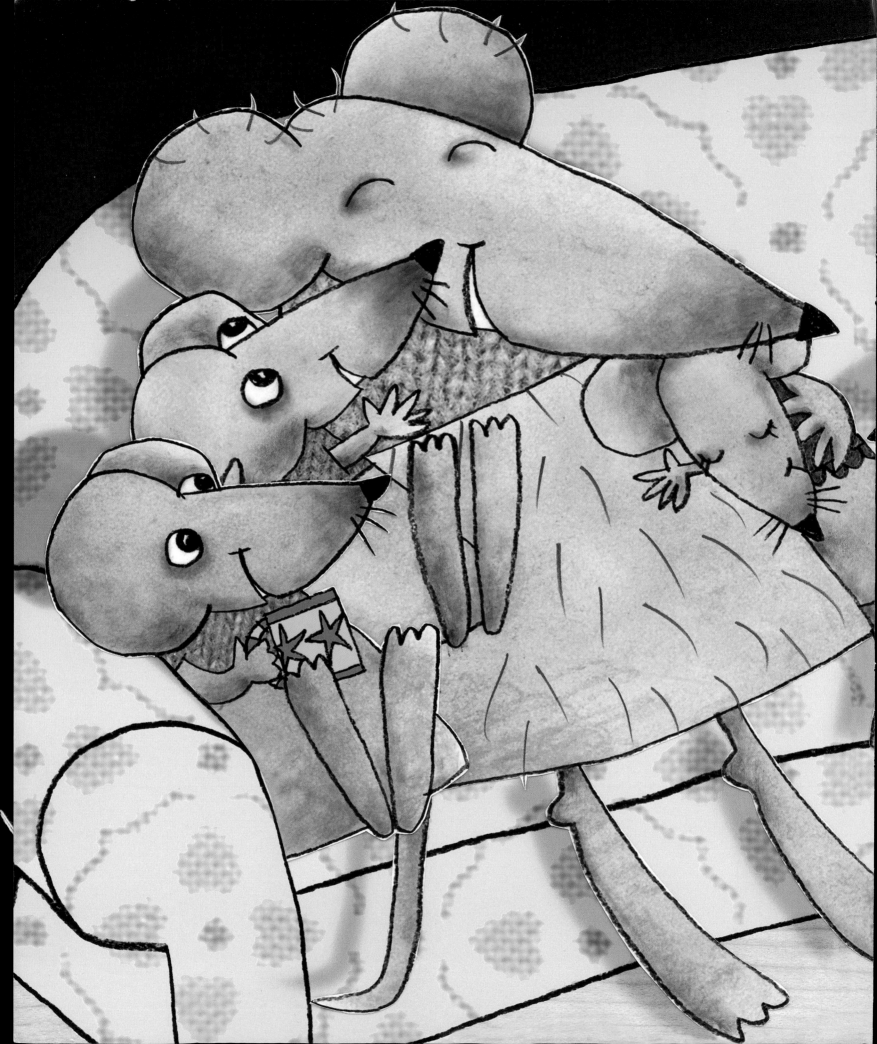

So Enormouse did.
He was back where
he truly belonged.

FRED

Clarissa

Tinymouse

ENORMOUSE